Dear Mr. Washington

Dear Mr. Washington

LYNN CULLEN
pictures by NANCY CARPENTER

Dial Books for Young Readers
an imprint of Penguin Group (USA) LLC

1st April, 1796

Dear Mr. Washington,

   I am Sorry for what happened to your hair Ribbon when you came to our house for Father to paint your Picture. James and I did not mean for our Cat to race up your Shoulder. Kitty was just Playing with Dash. (Dash is our Dog—I have drawn a Picture of him for you.)

And Baby John did not mean to chew your Ribbon. It only got a little Wet.

James and I just wanted to see if what Father said was true, that he could not get you to Smile for your Picture. You were not Smiling when James and I saw you. Not even when we gave you back your Ribbon.

Thank you for sending James and me the Book. They are Good Rules and I am copying them down, just like you said you did as a Boy. I am teaching them to James so you will come back, though they seem to Fly straight out of his head when he is around Baby John.

Here they are:

RULES OF GOOD BEHAVIOR FOR BOYS AND GIRLS

1. Do not be a Peacock, looking to See how nicely your Shoes and Stockings fit and how Handsome you are.

2. Do not run in the Streets nor go too slowly with your Mouth open . . .

. . . nor *Shake* your *Arms* nor kick the earth
nor go upon your *Toes* in a *Dancing fashion.*

3. **If** in the *Company* of someone **I**mportant,
walk behind him but in a manner that
he may easily *S*peak to you.

4. Make no Show in taking great Delight in your Food.

5. Put not another bite into your Mouth until the
first is Swallowed. Let not your Morsels be too big
for the Jowls, nor talk with your mouth Full.

6. *Do not Wiggle in the Sight of Others nor Gnaw your nails nor speak Louder than Ordinary.*

7. Do not Kill fleas, lice, and Ticks in the Sight of Others. If you see one upon your Companion, Pull it off privately. If it is upon your own Clothes, Thank him who pulls it off.

8. Do not be Curious to know the Business of Others.

9. Do not look Glad at the Misfortune of another.

10. Show Nothing to your Friend
that will frighten him.

In no time I am sure James and I will have learned all these Rules. I hope so, for Mother says until then we get no Pudding after dinner. And James and I love Chocolate Custard, even more than Baby John loves chewing on Shoes.

I hope you will come back soon so Father can finish your picture. You do not have to Smile if you do not want to. But if you did, you would look very Nice.

Sincerely,

Charlotte Stuart

8th April, 1796

Dear Mr. Washington,

James and I were so Glad when you came back to our House today. Father will paint such a pretty Picture of you, if only you will Smile. James and I thought if we were Very, Very Good, it might make you happier. So we followed the Rules very carefully.

Though Mother gave James new Stockings for your visit, he would not look at them.

When we saw your Carriage approach, we came
slowly as we could with our Arms tight at our
sides and our mouths Shut.

We followed you into the house far enough behind that you could not see Us, but we could hear you Speak. What is a "Scallywag"?

When Mother served Coffee & Cakes,
we were so very Polite. We only ate such
a Little Bit. Even Baby John sucked
quietly on your Shoe. I quietly picked off
my own Fleas—James did not try to see
how many—and he did not even Laugh
when I grew very Itchy. James could
have shown me the Spider hanging over
my head, making me jump with Fright,
but he did not.

We were so good, we were all soon fast Asleep. Even you.
Father is not happy. He says the Picture will never
be Finished at this rate.

So I ask again, Mr. Washington, won't
you please Come Back? We are getting better at the Rules
every day. And I know your picture will be Very, Very, Very
Nice. Even if you never Smile again.

Your Friend, Charlotte

15th April, 1796

Dear Mr. Washington,

James and I could not Believe it when your Carriage arrived today. Mother did not tell us you were Coming. She had told us to Play all we wanted, Far, Far Away. And to take Baby John. And Dash.

Imagine our Surprise when we came back because Baby John got Hungry and there you were!

We wanted to show you how much we had Learned, so that is why we insisted on giving you your Refreshments. We were quite Good, don't you think? Until Baby John wanted to see what was in the Bowl and dumped strawberry Punch all over himself. This is what comes of being Curious about the Business of Others.

But then James, who should have known better, forgot the Rules and laughed at Baby John's Misfortune.

Then I, knowing that James had broken the Rules and ruined your chances of ever Smiling, told him Father would put him out of the House forever. Without Dash.

That gave James such a Fright that he instantly began Crying until Dash
howled and Kitty ran and hid and Baby John broke into a loud, loud Wail.
What could I do but put Baby John on my Back and play Horsey, bucking and
whinnying until Baby John laughed?

So glad was I to make Baby John laugh, for a Minute I forgot You were there.
Then I remembered.

You were Smiling.

"You put me in mind of my favorite horse," you said, "stung by a honeybee."

Now Father's Picture is finished. It looks Very, Very, VERY Nice. But maybe you will like the Picture I am sending even Better. It is the best Horse I can do.

I hope you are still Smiling.

Love,
Charlotte

Author's Note

In April of 1796, George Washington, first president of the United States, came to the home of Gilbert Stuart, a famous artist, to have his portrait painted. Mr. Stuart's children, eventually twelve in all, most of whose names have been lost in history, witnessed this important event. But while their father had painted many portraits of famous people before, painting President Washington was different. President Washington *hated* having his picture painted. Mr. Stuart was in despair because Washington's grim expression was ruining the portrait. Not until Stuart struck upon talking about horses could he get Washington to smile. Washington *loved* horses. Though accounts differ as to how and when Stuart made this discovery (he painted three different portraits of Washington, one of which appears on the dollar bill), I like to imagine the Stuart children having a hand in it.

The fact remains that Washington did visit the Stuart household, though there is no record of how the Stuart children behaved. If they were like their father, they might have needed a book on good manners. Gilbert Stuart was known for his pranks and outrageous behavior.

Washington, on the other hand, was famous for his courtesy and excellent manners. He might well have learned them from a book he had to copy as a boy, *Rules of Civility & Decent Behavior in Company and Conversation*. The rules listed in *Dear Mr. Washington* are taken from this book, with the spelling and grammar modified for modern-day readers.

The picture the Stuart children saw their father paint in this story became one of the most famous of all the portraits made of George Washington. It is in the National Portrait Gallery in Washington, D.C.

For Keira
—L.C.

For my husband,
who breaks all the "Rules of Civility and Decent Behavior,"
but still keeps us all laughing.
—N.C.

DIAL BOOKS FOR YOUNG READERS
Published by the Penguin Group
Penguin Group (USA) LLC
375 Hudson Street, New York, NY 10014

USA / Canada / UK / Ireland / Australia / New Zealand / India / South Africa / China

penguin.com

A Penguin Random House Company

Library of Congress Cataloging-in-Publication Data
Cullen, Lynn.
Dear Mr. Washington / by Lynn Cullen ; pictures by Nancy Carpenter.
p.   cm.
Summary: In April, 1796, young Charlotte Stuart writes a series of letters to George Washington,
whose portrait is being painted by her father, reporting on her efforts and those of her brothers to follow
the rules of good behavior in the book Mr. Washington gave them. Includes historical notes.
ISBN 978-0-8037-3038-0 (hardcover)
[1. Behavior—Fiction. 2. Etiquette—Fiction. 3. Brothers and sisters—Fiction. 4. Letters—Fiction.
5. Washington, George, 1732-1799—Fiction. 6. Stuart, Gilbert, 1755-1828—Family—Fiction.]
I. Carpenter, Nancy, ill. II. Title.
PZ7.C8963De 2015 [Fic]—dc23   2012001098

George Washington (Lansdowne portrait) by Gilbert Stuart. Oil on canvas, 1796.
Photo courtesy of The National Portrait Gallery, Smithsonian Institution.
Manufactured in China on acid-free paper
1 3 5 7 9 10 8 6 4 2

Designed by Nancy R. Leo-Kelly
Text set in Oldbook ITC with Linotype Compendio Com Initials
The publisher does not have any control over and does not assume any responsibility for author or third-party websites or their content.

The art was prepared using a combination of pen on paper, acrylic paint on canvas, and digital media.